ALL HIS TOUCHES

STANDALONE DDLB ROMANCE

WEST GREENE

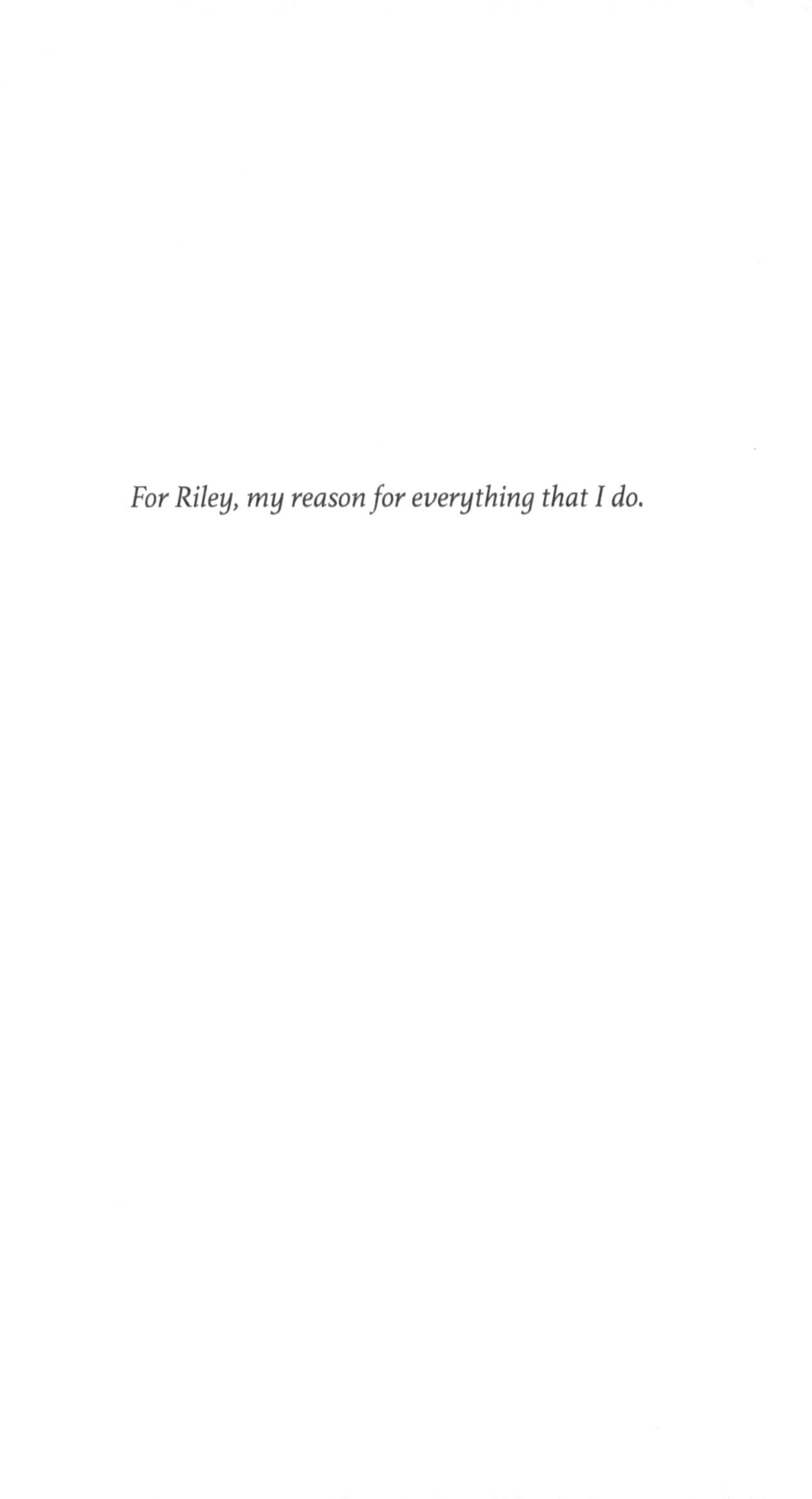

For Riley, my reason for everything that I do.

CHAPTER ONE

Forrest

I quietly stepped out of the bathroom after brushing my teeth, my eyes on my sweet boy. Brayden had rolled over onto his side, facing the side I usually slept on, and was cuddling my pillow to his chest, his face buried in the top of it. His curly hair —pink this week—was a mess on the top of his head, only serving to just make him look even more adorable.

We'd met when my foreman and best friend, Jax, forced me into the only salon in town that took walk-ins to get my hair cut before his wedding six months ago. I'd put it off until the last minute—took too long, too. Because there were no barbershops available to fit me in.

And there Brayden was, sweet as can be, bright blue curls dancing around his sweet, angel face as he spun to see who'd made the door jingle.

I'd almost crashed to my knees at the sight of him.

I hated being touched; trauma had fucked me up ten ways to Sunday in that capacity. Normally, if I allowed myself to even have sex, the guy I'd chosen for the night had to be tied up. Hence the reason I'd put off getting my hair cut for so long.

But then Brayden had cheerfully rang out a hello, his gorgeous, baby blue eyes sweeping over me, his pale cheeks burning red with a blush that stole my fucking heart. And I'd been a goner. I'd let him lead me to his chair and cut my hair and trim my beard and mustache, shaping me up for my best friend's wedding.

And before I realized what I'd been doing, I'd asked Brayden to be my date. And the cute as fuck way he'd stuttered, tripping over a simple yes, had captured my soul.

My sweet boy had wrecked me.

A month after our date, I practically forced him to move in with me, though he'd had zero complaints. I'd paid to break his lease, leaving his credit clean. I needed my boy with me whenever I could have him near. And though sometimes I still wasn't keen on being touched, I couldn't deny him—not when he looked at me with those big blue eyes and that sweet, hopeful smile, his curls —whatever color they happened to be that day—bouncing around his face.

Sighing softly, hating to leave him, especially when I knew beneath that comforter and sheet he was naked, his pretty little cock probably already waiting for me to grip him, I just brushed a light kiss to his lips, being careful not to wake him before I slipped from the room and headed into the kitchen to grab my lunch.

And just like it had been since the first morning I'd woken up for work after he moved in with me, my lunch was waiting for me on the counter, packed with two sandwiches, a soda, a bottle of water, an apple, and three cookies.

He really did take such damn good care of me.

Wishing I had time to go upstairs and thank my boy properly, I quickly shook my head and left the house, making sure to snatch up my lunch bag as I went.

I'd have plenty of time to thank my boy later tonight when we were both home and showered and no longer smelled like our jobs.

"Yo, boss, your boy is here!" one of my laborers called up to me.

Immediately, I shoved my hammer back into my tool belt and hurried down the ladder, turning to face where Brayden was standing, a hopeful look in his eyes, that adorable smile on his face.

"Daddy?" he called.

My heart clenched at the name. It'd weirded my employees out at first, hearing a boy call me Daddy, but they quickly warmed up to it, especially when they saw just how shy and timid he was.

It had slipped out of him one day, and when he'd panicked, thinking that wasn't what I wanted, I'd proceeded to slowly fuck him into my mattress until the only words spilling from his beautiful lips included Daddy.

"You okay, baby boy?" I asked, making my way to him. He was standing back from the construction area since he knew I'd rip him a new one for putting himself in danger. Fuck OSHA. I was the real nightmare when it came to his safety.

He nodded. "Can we eat lunch together?"

I glanced down at my watch and then back at my crew before whistling at them, grabbing their attention. "Lunch!" I shouted.

You'd think I'd just announced strippers were coming to give us our own personal show with the enthusiasm with which they moved and put their tools down.

Brayden reached for my hand and then stopped himself, looking up at me. "Can I, Daddy?"

In answer, I grabbed his hand in mine.

Since his hand was much smaller, I couldn't comfortably link our fingers together. But I did completely envelop his hand in mine, giving it a gentle squeeze as I led him over to my truck.

"My lunch, Daddy—"

He squeaked when I grabbed his waist and lifted him onto the tailgate. I brushed my hands up his thighs—he was wearing a tight pair of skinny jeans today that he knew would drive me wild—and brushed my lips with his in a teasing kiss that left him pouting at me, wanting more. "Stay," I ordered.

He quickly nodded his head and began to swing his legs, watching me as I walked over to his car and grabbed his lunch out of the passenger seat. After I grabbed mine, I hopped up into the truck and then pulled him between my legs, my back resting against the back of the bed.

"Comfy?" I asked him, handing him his food.

He nodded. "Always comfortable with you, Daddy."

I brushed a light kiss to his neck in response.

Touching him was easy some days. Others, when I hit lows, I struggled. But my boy never let me feel bad for what I couldn't give him all the time. I knew he thrived on physical touch, but he always assured me he was okay and happy with whatever I could give him.

"How come you didn't let me know you were coming?" I asked him once my food was finished and he was lounging back against my chest, his eyes shut, my arms wrapped tightly around him.

"Wanted to surprise you," he said. "Zarrie is being a righteous bitch today, too, and I just needed my Daddy."

I rested my chin on the top of his head, anger stirring in my chest at the thought of someone ruining his day, even if it was his boss. "I'm always here if you need me," I quietly reminded him.

He turned his head and pressed a kiss to my arm, which I knew was dirty and sweaty, but he didn't seem to mind.

"I know, Daddy," he said softly. "That's why I came."

This boy.

CHAPTER TWO

Brayden

Zarrie scowled at me. "There's still a piece of hair on the floor," she griped, pointing at it. I clenched my hand around the broom, blinking back tears. I was so tired and frustrated. She was being so rude and mean today, and I didn't understand why.

Okay, maybe I did. I knew she'd caught her husband cheating, but God, did she have to take out her bad mood on everyone else?

The news of her husband cheating had spread around the salon like wildfire when he'd had the audacity to come in with roses and her favorite food, begging for her forgiveness in front of all the clients we had in the shop. Her mood had only gotten worse after he did that. And I still had a small headache from all her screaming.

"I'm working on it," I quietly told her.

She snatched the broom from my hand. "Just go home, Brayden," she griped.

Tears clogged my throat. I was a baby—sue me. My feelings always easily got hurt, and I hated it. I wanted to be like other guys and be able to stand my ground and tell her what a bitch she was being, but instead, I quickly rushed to the back, trying to hide my tears so she wouldn't see them.

Sniffling, I swiped my sleeve under my nose and grabbed my zebra print bag that Forrest had bought me two months ago as a random gift, shoving it onto my shoulder. Nessa suddenly stepped up and wrapped me in a hug, rubbing my back. Nessa was always so nice to me.

"Go home and get some rest. Maybe tomorrow will be better," she whispered.

Sniffling, I nodded my head and quickly clocked out before leaving out the back door even faster. Once I was in my car, I texted Forrest like I always did, letting him know I was on my way home. He tracked the time—and sometimes my location—to make sure I was safe. And while I knew some people thought it was overbearing—like Nessa, for example, who was the closest thing I had to a best friend—I loved it. I loved that he took care of me like this.

When I got home, I stared at the kitchen, knowing I should get dinner in the oven, but I just couldn't seem to muster up the strength to do so. Instead, I just shot off my text to Forrest, letting him know I was home safe, locked the front door, and then trudged up the stairs to our room.

Normally, I got a shower after I got dinner in the oven so I didn't smell like hair chemicals, but I didn't have the energy after the day I'd had today.

My phone rang, breaking me from my thoughts. Forrest's picture popped up on the screen. I quickly swiped my thumb across my phone, answering his call and putting on speaker. "Yes, Daddy?" I asked, my voice sounding tired and weak to my own ears.

"Saw you on the cameras," he said. I forgot he had those in the house; they're part of his security system. He had them before I moved in, and though he'd warned me about them, I always forgot. Besides, it didn't bother me to have him watching me all the time. "You okay, sweet boy?"

I sighed and sat down on the edge of the bed, dropping my zebra bag by my feet. "Zarrie upset me," I said quietly.

"What'd she do, baby boy?" His voice was low and dark, his overprotectiveness kicking into high gear. He didn't play around when it came to my feelings and emotions.

I sighed. "Daddy, it's—"

"If you say it's okay..." he growled, warning me to tread carefully. "Nothing that upsets you this much is okay, Brayden." The use of my full name had me swallowing thickly. Daddy meant business.

"Her husband cheated on her, and he blasted it in front of the entire salon and all the clients there at the time when he came in with roses and her favorite food to beg for her forgiveness," I found myself spilling. "Her mood went from bad to worse, and while I was cleaning up today at closing, I guess I didn't sweep up a piece of hair fast enough for her, and she just snatched the broom from me and sent me home."

He growled. "Get a shower, boy."

With that, he hung up. I swallowed thickly and glanced at my screen, watching as it went black. I had no doubt in my mind he'd be calling Zarrie and giving her a piece of his mind. The last time she'd done something like this, he had done exactly that, and the next day, she was apologizing to me and buying me lunch.

Forrest knew I sucked at sticking up for myself, but he constantly told me he was there to protect me, too. I just wish I wasn't such a cry baby and could do it myself. But confrontation freaked me out.

Sighing, I got off the bed and trudged to the bathroom, following my Daddy's orders. Even if I didn't feel like showering and instead just wanted to crawl into bed, I'd do as he said because if there was one thing in this world that could cheer me up, even if only just a little, it was pleasing Daddy.

CHAPTER THREE

Forrest

I rang the salon three times before someone finally picked up. It was after closing, but I wasn't stupid. I knew Zarrie would still be there, counting drawers, and getting money ready to deposit into the bank in the morning.

"We're closed," she said into the phone. I could tell she was forcing herself to be nice.

"Don't care," I bit out. She sucked in a sharp breath of air. "When my boy comes back in that salon in the morning for work, Zarrie, you owe him a major apology. Not only did you hurt his feelings for no reason, but he also cried. That boy does everything in the world to please all of you there. He didn't deserve the day you've given him."

She sighed softly, sounding tired and worn down, but I didn't care how she felt—not after what she'd done to my sweet boy. Seeing his teary eyes and red face on that fucking camera had almost made me throw the tool in my fucking hand.

"I'm sorry, Forrest. It's been a rough day," she said quietly.

"Don't apologize to me. Save your apologies for him—and probably the rest of your employees, too, yeah?"

"Yeah," she agreed. "I'll talk to him tomorrow, and I'll make it up to him."

We ended the call, and I started up my truck, heading home to my boy. My last look at the camera had shown him curled up in bed, his pink curls hanging damp around his face, his eyes locked on some romance movie on TV.

When I got home, he was still curled up in bed. I pressed a kiss to his temple. "Give me five minutes to get a shower," I quietly told him.

He just nodded. I brushed my hand over his soft curls and then strode to the bathroom, quickly stripping off my clothes and stepping into the shower, washing the dirt and grime off my body. My mind went to my boy as I scrubbed at my skin and washed my hair and beard, wondering what I could do to cheer him up. Now that I was agitated, the thought of anyone touching me made my skin crawl, but I knew he needed to feel me when he was like this.

Fuck, how did we work so well when half the time, I struggled to give him everything he needed? It made me feel like such a shitty fucking Daddy. He deserved better than me.

Heaving a sigh I hoped my boy couldn't hear, I stepped out of the shower and wrapped a towel around my waist before my eyes landed on my tub. It was pretty fucking big, and jets shot out of the side even after the water was off, keeping it the perfect temperature, so whoever was soaking could stay there as long as they wanted. Brayden loved that tub, and suddenly, I knew exactly what I was going to do.

Pulling up his favorite movie—*Pretty*

Woman—on the bathroom wall across from the tub—but not above it because like fuck would I risk the TV falling into the tub with Brayden—I paused it at the beginning and then began running a bath for him, pouring in his favorite lavender-scented bath stuff.

I stepped into the room. "Baby boy," I called, drawing his eyes to me. His eyes swept over me, hunger sparking in his gaze before he focused those darkened blues on my face. "Come here," I ordered.

He immediately moved out of bed, a pair of his favorite lacey panties on with one of my t-shirts almost falling to his mid-thigh. He came to a stop in front of me, his fingers linked together in front of him, his head tilted back to look at me.

"Let's get a bath," I told him. "We'll soak for a while, and once you're feeling better, we'll order some food. Sound good?"

He nodded. I gestured for him to move ahead of me, and once we were in the bathroom, his eyes brightened a bit. "*Pretty Woman*?" he asked, unable to contain the little bit of excitement in his voice. He knew the movie got on my nerves, but this boy still had yet to realize I'd do anything in the world for him if it meant keeping him happy.

I'd rip out my own heart, slash my own soul, if it meant he kept smiling at me.

"Get undressed, baby."

He quickly stripped out of his clothes, and I quickly grabbed his hands, not wanting him to slip as he stepped into the tub. He sighed as he sank down into it, his eyes softly closing. I dropped my towel and stepped in as well, taking a seat across from him. He slowly opened his eyes, locking them on mine.

"You okay, Daddy?"

"Just angry that someone upset my boy," I told him quietly. "I don't like seeing you upset."

He frowned, seeming conflicted, though I knew his feelings were still hurt. "She just had a bad day—"

"Aht," I growled, cutting him off. His eyes snapped to mine. Now, I was angry for an entirely different reason. I hated it when he tried making excuses for someone else's shitty behavior, especially when that person *hurt* him. "Come here—*now*," I ordered.

He quickly moved and straddled my legs. I was too focused on him for my body to react to him touching me in a negative way. In fact, when his pert little ass settled snuggly over my cock, I wanted to do nothing more than slide up into him.

I gripped his pink curls, tightening my grip until he whimpered, his blue fingernails digging into my shoulders. "Do we make excuses for people making you feel like shit?" I asked him.

He trembled beneath the roughness in my voice as it washed over his skin. "No, Daddy."

"Then why are you making excuses for Zarrie?" I demanded.

He swallowed thickly. "I feel bad for her," he whispered.

I pulled his face close to mine, to the point our lips just barely brushed. My eyes never left his even as my cock jumped in response to those sweet lips being so, so fucking close to mine.

"Feeling bad for her does not give you a reason to excuse her behavior, Brayden," I reminded him. "I have half a mind to paint your pretty ass red, you hear me? Don't do it again."

He tried to nod, but I was holding him too tightly. "Okay, Daddy. I won't. I promise."

I released his hair and tugged his body against my chest, leaning down to claim his lips with mine, soothing him after being rough with him. He sighed into the kiss, his addictive lips parting for me, allowing me to thrust my tongue into his warm, wet mouth.

He whimpered into the kiss, his ass grinding against my cock. I slid my hand down his spine before probing at his taint, brushing my finger over it. He trembled, gasping into my mouth before moaning and bearing down on my finger, easily allowing me inside of him.

"Such a naughty boy," I rasped.

He shook his head, panting, his eyes blissed out as I slowly fucked him with my finger. "I only want to be your good boy, Daddy."

I nipped at his jaw, gently adding a second finger to the first. His lips parted, his eyes rolling back in his head. "You're always my good boy," I promised him. "But sometimes, even good boys are naughty in all the right ways."

His head fell to my shoulder, and he panted against my skin as I picked up the pace of my fingers, finally allowing myself to brush against his prostate. He cried out, his hands tightening on me before sliding around my shoulders, grinding down against me.

"Daddy," he whimpered. "I need—I want—"

I added a third finger, and the erotic sound that ripped from his throat had my cock weeping. I pumped my fingers in and out of him, stretching him, prepping him for my cock. I hadn't even pressed play on the movie yet, but it didn't seem like I was going to need it.

"Daddy," he pleaded, whining low in his throat. "I need to come, Daddy."

I pulled my fingers out of him and then stood out of the water with his little body wrapped around me. Not even bothering with a towel, I stepped into our bedroom and laid him out on the bed. He wiggled, reaching for me, but I stayed out of his reach, instead reaching over to my nightstand to grab the bottle of lube.

He looked so fucking beautiful as he watched me slick my cock up, his eyes so dark they were almost black, his pupils blown. He was breathing heavily, like he'd just run a marathon. And I knew he was anticipating what he knew I could do to his body.

He used to be so shy with me, but now he never hesitated to beg and plead for me to fuck him, to make him come. And I loved the needy words that always spilled from his lips when we were together.

I slicked up my fingers and gently eased them inside of him, spreading him apart. His back arched, his eyes rolling back in his head when I brushed over that spot inside of him. His skinny cock jumped and leaked precum on his belly. "Daddy, please!" he cried, on the verge of sobbing for me.

"You sure you're ready for me?" I teased, a wicked smirk on my lips. I loved teasing him, keeping him right there on the edge, so needy and desperate for my cock inside of him.

"P-please," he stuttered as I let my finger drift over that sensitive spot again. He moved to wrap his hand around his pretty prick, but I growled and smacked it away. This time, a sob ripped from his throat at the same time a tear ran down his cheek.

I loved to see him cry for me like this.

I pulled my fingers out of him and then replaced them with my cock. "Oh, God," he cried out, his back bowing off the bed, his hands pulling at his hair.

"That's right, boy. I'm your god," I growled, sliding out and pushing back in a little rougher, just the way my sweet boy loved.

"So full," he whimpered.

I grunted, pulling out and shoving back in, screwing him into the mattress.

"Daddy," he sobbed, tears tracking down his cheeks. I loved that he cried every time I fucked him. He got so lost in everything he felt when we were joined together like this— the love, me stuffing him full of my cock, the intense need to come. It was fucking beautiful.

"You want more?" I taunted, still easing in

and out of him with just that tiny little bit of punch to my thrusts—just enough to brush his prostate every time, but not enough to make him come.

"Pl-please," he begged, his eyes locking on mine. I gripped his hips to the point I knew my grip just might leave bruises. But they were the only marks I'd ever put on my boy's skin. "I need it, Daddy."

I leaned over him and licked up some of his tears, loving how salty they tasted on my tongue. "These tears for me, boy?"

He nodded, wrapping his arms around my shoulders. I licked up another one before leaning up and finally giving him what he was begging me for.

I pushed his knees further back, spreading his perky ass farther apart for me, and began to thrust hard and fast inside his tight ass. He cried out my name, and just like he always did, he came without a single touch to his cock, spilling across his chest and stomach. With my free hand, the one not gripping his thigh like my fucking life depended on it, I smeared his cum all over his chest.

My balls began to draw up tight, and I growled. "Where do you want me to come, pretty boy?"

"On me," he begged. "Come on me, Daddy."

I pulled out of him at the last second and gripped my cock, giving it two hard strokes before my cum splashed all over his chest, belly, and neck, mixing with his.

He trembled, gasping for air as he smeared my cum with his, officially marking himself as mine like he loved to do.

I leaned forward, not giving a fuck about the cum covering him, and took his lips in a slow, sweet kiss. "See? Good boys can be naughty in all the good ways," I rasped.

He just dazedly smiled up at me, completely dicked out.

CHAPTER FOUR

I groaned as I brushed my teeth, pain lancing through my stomach. After eating dinner, Brayden barely keeping his eyes open through it all, we'd crashed, tired and worn out from both work and sex. But then, my needy boy, at about three this morning, had tentatively woken me up with his hand on my cock, and when I'd groaned and thrust into his hand, he'd climbed on top of me and eased me inside him, slowly riding me until we were coming together.

Flinching as more pain pushed through my stomach, I quickly finished brushing my teeth and then took some gas pills, hoping that eased the pain. Maybe the pizza we'd eaten last night wasn't agreeing with me, though I'd never had an issue before.

I brushed my lips lightly with my boy's before slipping quietly down the stairs, my boots barely making any noise as I moved toward the kitchen, surprised to see my lunch sitting on the counter. A small smile pulled at my lips. I had no idea when he'd slipped down here to make it, but he'd had to be a sneaky little thing to accomplish it, considering I usually noticed the moment he slipped from my arms.

God, I didn't deserve a boy like him.

I grabbed it off the counter and then headed to the front door, my stomach pinching with pain again. Biting back a curse, knowing exactly what kind of hell awaited me trying to work with a stomach ache, I locked the front door back behind me and headed to my truck, hoping like hell those gas pills kicked in and did something to relieve the pain.

I threw up in the grass a few feet from the house we were working on building. It was the third time I'd thrown up, and this time when pain pulsed through my lower stomach, I almost went crashing to my knees.

Something was really fucking wrong.

"Brother, I think you need a doctor," Jax said, coming up beside me with a bottle of water. He held it out to me, but I pushed it away, the mere thought of trying to swallow something—even if it was water—making me want to throw up again.

"Call off work," I grunted, bending at the waist when the pain in my stomach just continued to intensify. "Get me to the hospital."

He nodded. Thankfully, he didn't seem alarmed or freaked out—ever the calm one. "Come on. Let's get you in my truck first," he said, supporting some of my weight. I could barely walk anymore.

Brayden was going to flip out when he heard about this, and my heart squeezed in my chest. I needed to be there for my boy, but I couldn't until I knew what in the hell was going on. "Do *not* call Brayden," I told Jax, groaning in pain afterward. "Let me find out what's going on first."

Jax sighed. "He's going to be angry with you, Forrest."

I shook my head. "Let him be angry, but at least he won't panic over a thousand what-ifs," I bit out, easing myself into the passenger seat of his truck. "Call off work," I ordered again.

He nodded and rushed off, getting everyone cleared off the job site. I threw up again before he was able to make it back to the truck. He grimaced as he dodged the vomit on the ground. "I hope it's only food poisoning."

I doubted it was, but it would be nice if it were something as simple as that. But Brayden would have to be sick, too, and he wasn't. I knew he wasn't because he'd be calling me crying if he felt like this, begging me to make him feel better.

My heart twisted with pain at the mere thought of him feeling this agony. I dealt with pain well, and if I was hurting this bad?

They'd have to sedate Brayden for him to cope with it.

When we got to the hospital, Jax helped me get checked in, and then we waited for what felt like forever for someone to come get me into a triage room. I threw up two more times, now throwing up nothing but stomach acid. I felt like absolute hell was wreaking havoc on my body.

"Forrest Dallas?" a feminine voice called out.

Jax helped me to my feet, and with his help, I made my way to the smiling, blonde nurse. She frowned when she ran her eyes over me. "Come on. I'll make this fast," she promised me.

I just nodded my head, following her instructions and answering her questions as she took my weight, blood pressure, pulse, and temperature. "You're not running a fever," she said quietly, typing the temp into her computer. "Sit tight, hun. I'm going to see if we have a room open for you, and then I'm going to do my best to get the doctor in to see you as soon as possible, okay?"

"Sounds good," I grunted, leaning forward since bending my body in half seemed to at least alleviate *some* of the pain.

Jax sighed. "Brayden texted," he told me quietly.

I looked up at him, not even realizing he had my phone. I held out my hand, and he handed it over to me. I typed in my passcode and smiled at the pic he sent me. He was in the bathroom at work, his curls perfectly styled, his blue eyes bright with happiness as he smiled into the mirror for me.

BRAYDEN

Thinking of you, Daddy. I
love you.

Oh, my sweet, cuddly, baby boy. For just a tiny moment, my pain was forgotten as I smiled at his picture and his message. I really loved this boy so fucking much.

I love you, too, sweet boy.

I handed Jax back my phone and dragged the nearest trashcan to me, vomiting into it right as the nurse walked in. As soon as I was done, she called for someone to come take out the trash and then led me to a room. "The doctor will be in soon, okay?"

I just nodded, gritting my teeth against the pain.

Surgery. Appendicitis. Hours away from bursting.

That was all that was running through my mind as I listened to the doctor and his plan for me. Brayden was going to freak out. He wasn't going to be able to handle this.

Fuck.

I rubbed my hands down my face, trying to think past the pain meds they were pushing into my system through the IV. I was getting sleepy, and I needed to talk to my boy. Jax already had power of attorney over my health, but I knew he'd make any choices Brayden told him to over my health when it came down to it.

"I need to make a phone call," I told him, my words already slurring.

The doctor nodded. "I'll be back in a bit," he assured me.

Jax handed me my phone, and I called Brayden's work number. Nessa answered, but when she realized it was me, she quickly put Brayden on the phone.

"Daddy?" he asked, sounding alarmed. *Fuck. Fuck!* I didn't want him scared—not before he got here safely. "Daddy, what's wrong?"

"Need you to come to the hospital," I told him. His sharp intake of air made my heart hurt worse than my stomach had been. "Be a big boy for just a little while, okay? And get here safely, you hear me?"

I knew he had a million questions on the tip of his tongue, but he was my good boy. He'd do as I said. "Okay, Daddy. I love you. I love you a lot."

"I love you, too, baby. Drive safe."

I ended the call and let my eyes slide shut, too tired to fight against the morphine in my system anymore.

CHAPTER FIVE

"Zarrie," I called, rushing into her office. She looked up at me in alarm. I was sure she could hear the panic in my voice. I was freaking out. Forrest was in the hospital, and he sounded bad—really bad. Something was wrong with my Daddy. It felt like I could barely breathe.

"Take a deep breath," she ordered, quickly standing up from her desk. I did, but barely. It hurt to breathe without him grounding me. "Tell me what's going on, Brayden."

I sank my teeth into my bottom lip,

drawing blood. I grimaced at the metallic taste, but it distracted me for a moment from the mess in my head, the panic, the fear that Daddy might not make it.

Oh, God.

"Daddy—hospital," I managed to get out.

She quickly grabbed my hand and her keys before leading me out of her office, shutting the door behind her. "You're in no condition to drive." She led me out into the sea of other employees and clients. "Nessa, please hold down the fort until I can get back."

Nessa frowned at me, concern flashing in her eyes. "Brayden?"

Tears washed in my eyes, and when she reached out for me, I shook my head. I didn't want anyone but Daddy hugging me right now.

Somehow, I ended up in the passenger seat of Zarrie's car. I didn't remember how I got there. And then just as fast, it seemed like we were at the hospital, and I had no recollection of the drive. My mind was running rampant with fear.

I couldn't live this life without Daddy by my side. I needed him like I needed air to breathe. Fuck, Daddy was my air. Without him, I didn't exist.

"Come on, hun," Zarrie soothed, helping me out of her car. She led me inside, and then Jax, Daddy's best friend, was there taking over, thanking her before curling his massive arm around my shoulder and leading me down a few hallways until he pushed open a door, revealing Daddy's sleeping form.

He was so pale, his lips having lost their color. His clothes were neatly folded on a chair, and a hospital gown covered his body. I whimpered, rushing forward to grab his hand. "Daddy?" I whimpered, hot tears streaking down my cheeks, ruining the mascara I'd carefully applied this morning.

"Hold on," Jax soothed. He gently shook Daddy until he blinked sleepily at us, groaning low in his throat when he moved. "Hey, Forrest. Your boy is here."

Daddy's eyes slowly focused on me, and sadness sprang into their dark depths. "Come here, boy."

I curled onto the bed beside him, and he tucked me against him, holding me there.

"Breathe. When you calm down, I'll tell you what's wrong," he told me, his words slow and chosen carefully. I inhaled the scent of him—spice and laundry detergent mixed with a slight bit of sweat. My heart rate slowly calmed until I was breathing normally again.

"Daddy, what's happening?" I quietly asked him, tracing designs onto his chest.

He brushed his lips to the top of my head. "I have appendicitis. We caught it in time." I listened intently, trying not to freak out again. He was talking slowly, which made it hard, but with me wrapped in his arms, his steady heartbeat beneath my ear, I was able to ground myself. "I'll have surgery in a little bit. They'll take out my appendix, and then I'll be okay again."

I trembled. "You promise?" I croaked, tears building in my eyes again. He was going to be cut open. How was he so calm?

He brushed his lips to the top of my head. "I promise, baby boy. Nothing will take me away from you unless it's old age, you hear me?"

I nodded my head against his chest. He ran his hand over my pink curls. "I love you."

I sniffled, doing my best to hold in my tears. "I love you more than anything in the world, Daddy."

Jax held my hand in his as they wheeled Daddy out of the room he was in, taking him to the OR. Once he was gone, disappearing down the hall, a nurse led us to the waiting room for family waiting for patients in the operating room, leaving us with the promise that Daddy was in good hands and the surgeon would come to speak to us as soon as Daddy was in recovery.

"Do you think Daddy will be okay?" I asked Jax, terrified of his answer.

He squeezed his arm around my shoulder. "Forrest is not leaving you, Brayden. Remember that. Pretty sure I've overheard him reminding you of who's your god when you two sneak off when I come over with Tyson sometimes."

I flushed red and covered my face with

my hands. Jax just chuckled. "If that man believes he's your god, then trust in him, yeah? He said he wasn't leaving you. Believe in that."

I nodded and rested my head on his shoulder, curling my knees to my chest.

And we waited.

CHAPTER SIX

Forrest

I was pretty out of it my first few hours in the hospital after surgery. I spent most of the time asleep, my hand wrapped around Brayden's. Once the anesthesia began to wear off a good bit, they let me go home, and now, I was watching my boy flit around the house, jittery and unsure of what to do with himself.

I knew he was craving my touch, and with the pain I was in, I wasn't sure if I could take it. But fuck, I hated seeing him like this. My boy had just gone through something traumatic. He'd thought he was losing me. Shit, Jax had informed me Zarrie had to drive him to the hospital because he was panicking and freaking out after I called him and told him to come to me.

I yawned, my eyes sliding shut. I'd be glad when the pain got manageable enough to go without the oxycodone. Because I hated sleeping all the time, especially when Brayden was like this. He needed me alert, and right now, I wasn't even fit to take care of him.

"Baby boy," I gruffly called, my voice heavily tinged with sleep. He immediately stopped wiping down the counters from our dinner, turning those stunning, blue eyes on me. With a grunt, I pushed myself off the couch. "Let's go to bed. I'm tired."

Immediately, he was by my side. He wasn't touching me; I was pretty sure he could sense I wasn't in the headspace for that, but I felt his presence wrap around me, somehow soothing us both the tiniest little bit.

Climbing the stairs was absolute hell, but

I managed it. But by the end of it, I was seriously internally cursing myself for buying a fucking house where all the bedrooms were upstairs—not a single room downstairs. The fuck *had* I been thinking?

Certainly not of anyone having surgery; that was for sure.

I eased onto the bed with a grunt. "Daddy, let me help you," Brayden pleaded when I tried to peel my shirt over my head, grunting with the movement.

I looked up at him. He looked so miserable, and it fucking wrecked my goddamn soul. I nodded, and he quickly walked over to me, gently grabbing the bottom of my t-shirt before he pulled it over my head, barely hurting me. His hands hovered over the button on my jeans, and after giving him a single nod in permission, he unbuttoned them and slid them down my legs before pulling my socks off with them.

I eased back onto the bed, sighing in relief once I was on my side and comfortable, the strain taken off my surgery site. They'd had to do one long incision instead of doing a microscopic surgery like they'd normally do since my appendix was so swollen.

"I'm going to get a shower, Daddy. Do you need anything?" Brayden quietly asked me.

I shook my head, already falling asleep. "Be careful, baby boy." All I could picture was him accidentally falling or slipping in the shower, and my heart raced in panic at the thought of not being able to help him.

Christ, I hated this shit.

"I will, Daddy. I promise."

I nodded and drifted of to sleep, no longer able to fight the effects of the medication I was on.

I flicked my eyes to the kitchen, where Brayden was banging around, doing God only knew what. He'd taken two weeks off to be with me while I recovered, and while we'd already been through week one and I was doing much better, he was still worried sick about me. The house had been cleaned five times already, the kitchen was so spotless, I was surprised the damn walls didn't somehow shine and show me my reflection, and we had so many cookies and pies, I was pretty sure over half of them were going to end up going bad before either of us could ever eat them.

I left him alone though. This was how he coped with things he couldn't control, and I wouldn't take that from him. Sighing, I focused back on the football game playing, frowning when I realized that while I'd been distracted by my sweet boy, the team I was rooting for had somehow lost the fucking ball.

Dimwits.

I lifted my mug of coffee to my lips and took a sip before setting it back down, watching as the opposing team got closer and closer to the touchdown line.

What a sorry-ass game.

Suddenly realizing the house was quiet besides the TV playing the game, I looked around for my boy, not finding him. I frowned. "Brayden?" I called, hoping he wasn't somewhere lost in his head, thinking he couldn't come seek comfort from me. I'd always put aside how I was feeling for him.

He came down the stairs a minute later, a blanket I hadn't seen him use in months wrapped around his shoulders. Before he moved in with me, he slept with that blanket every night; it was his security blanket. And my heart squeezed in my chest at the sight of it.

He was using it because I wasn't giving him what he needed, and fuck if that didn't gut me.

And that smile I loved to see from him was missing, breaking my heart even more.

I fucking hated this shit. I never wanted him to feel like this.

With a soft sigh, I leaned back against the armrest of the couch and rested one leg on the floor, creating room between my body and the back of the couch. I wasn't a small guy by any means, but I'd make it work. My boy fucking needed me, and I'd neglected his needs damn long enough.

"Come here," I gently ordered, curling four of my fingers to beckon him to me with my left hand.

He slowly made his way to me and

stopped beside my leg, a frown pulling at his lips. "What's wrong, Daddy?"

His voice sounded small, and I fucking hated it. He was always supposed to be my happy, sweet boy, and I was hurting him.

"Get over here," I told him, patting the back of the couch.

He frowned. "But Daddy—"

I growled, the sound a warning that he better not argue with me. A small smile tugged at his lips. He fought it, but inevitably, that smile won out, brightening his eyes the tiniest bit. Without another word, he laid down between me and the back of the couch, resting his head on my bulky chest, a sigh of contentment leaving his lips. I wrapped my arm around him, pressing my lips to the top of his head.

Even my own body was relaxing beneath him. Guess I needed this, too; just hadn't realized it. Shouldn't be all that surprised though. I always needed my boy.

"If you need me, come to me," I quietly told him, the game long forgotten now that he was curled up in my hold, getting what he needed from me.

He pressed a kiss to my bare chest, and a shiver wracked down my spine. I barely bit back a groan. I'd missed having those lips on my body.

"You didn't want to be touched lately," he said quietly in explanation.

I sighed, shaking my head. I'd always shove past that need to not be touched if he needed me. How did he not realize that yet?

"What did I just say, boy?" I questioned him, using my right hand to push his curls out of his face so I had a clear view of those baby blue eyes.

He just smiled and snuggled closer to me, being careful of my incision. "To come to you if I need you, Daddy," he quietly answered.

I pressed another kiss to the top of his head. "Good boy. Don't forget that, you hear me?"

He nodded, his eyes fluttering shut. No doubt, he hadn't been sleeping well for the last week, but I'd thought it was because he was overly conscious of trying not to hurt me in his sleep.

Maybe he'd just been starved of my touch.

I'd been a really shitty Daddy the past few days, but I'd make sure this shit didn't happen again.

My sweet boy's needs always came before my own.

CHAPTER SEVEN

I was on a small boat that had hit some choppy waves, and Brayden was whimpering in fear, terrified we would flip over. But he had to know I'd never put him in harm's way, right? I had control of the boat; he was okay. I was okay.

"Daddy," my boy whimpered. "Oh, fuck."

My eyes snapped open. Darkness enveloped our bedroom, but I could make out my boy thrusting into his hand, his eyes squeezed shut as he quietly panted, needing to come but not able to. His body was covered in a light sheen of sweat, his plump lips parted, his pretty cock leaking precum, slicking up his hand.

I released a soft growl, and his eyes snapped open, his head jerking over to me. He sank his teeth into his bottom lip, his hand stilling, his hips frozen in place.

I arched a brow at him. "You had me dreaming we were in a boat, naughty one."

His cheeks flushed red in embarrassment. I rolled over and flicked on the lamp, snatching the bottle of lube from the night-stand afterward. He licked his lips when he noticed what I had. "Daddy, you don't—I'm okay—"

"Quiet, boy," I murmured, squeezing some lube on my fingers. "Come closer."

He quickly moved so he was pressed against me. I rolled him onto his side and hiked his leg over my thighs so he was spread open for me. His prick was leaking between us, still so hard and needing relief.

Even if I couldn't fuck him into the mattress like I so badly wanted to do, I could still get him off. I could give him this. I could relieve that ache in his balls and send him flying off that cliff into bliss.

"You ready for me?" I rasped, brushing my fingers over his taint, slicking him up just the tiniest bit.

He whimpered and nodded, his hands flattened on my chest between us, his hot breath fanning across my chest as he waited for me to breach him where he wanted me so badly.

I sank a finger inside of him, groaning at how tight he was. He whimpered, bearing down, opening himself up more for me, easily allowing me to sink in another finger. I thrust them in and out of him, wishing I could fuck him as hard and fast as I usually did with my cock. And sure, I could have used the dildo I'd bought him a couple of months ago, but I needed to feel him like this.

"Daddy," he pleaded. "More. I need more."

I wasn't going to deny him anything tonight. I slid another finger in, stretching him wide before I rolled him to his back. He kept his knees up in the air for me, allowing me to continue pumping my fingers in and out of him, brushing his prostate with every other stroke as I moved between his thighs.

"Oh, God," he whimpered, his chest heaving, his lower belly becoming slick with his precum. "I'm so close, Daddy."

I dipped my head and took his cock into my mouth. He cried out, his back bowing off the bed, his fingers tightening around the back of his knees. I sucked him to the back of my throat, swallowing around him before I swirled my tongue over his head, moaning at the taste of him.

He sobbed, his body trembling. I had him right there on the edge and with one, two, three strokes of his prostate while swallowing around his cock, he came down my throat with a scream, his body shaking, hot tears streaking down his beautiful face.

I eased my fingers out of him and then laid back down beside him, pulling him into my arms, brushing my clean hand over his hair until his crying ceased and his trembling stopped.

"You good, baby?" I quietly asked him, brushing my lips to the top of his head.

He weakly nodded his head. "Thank you,

Daddy." He brushed his fingers over my cock, but I gently pulled them away. I didn't get him off to get the same in return. I wanted to please my boy and make him feel good again.

"Not tonight, sweet boy. This was all for you." I pressed my lips lightly to his, soothing my tongue over his swollen bottom lip that he'd obviously been biting on. "Let me get cleaned up, and then I'll come cuddle you. Sound good?"

A sleepy smile pulled at his lips. "Sounds perfect, Daddy."

I eased from the bed and made my way to the bathroom. By the time I had my hands cleaned and had made my way back to bed, my boy was already asleep, soft snores leaving his lips. I softly smiled at him before sliding into bed beside him, pulling him into my arms, cuddling him just as I promised I would.

"I love you, baby boy," I whispered, brushing my lips to his forehead.

A light snore was all the response I got, and it had me smiling wider than I had in days.

CHAPTER EIGHT

Forrest

Normalcy had never felt so fucking good.

I was finally back at work, no longer on light duty at that, so I was able to get back into the swing of things. Light duty had driven me up the fucking wall, and numerous times, I'd gone home agitated because I couldn't do everything I wanted to, and instead had to stand back and watch everyone fucking do it for me.

Brayden, bless his sweet soul, had cuddled me on the couch or in bed each night, soothing me. And every night, I got him off, leaving him a beautiful, crying mess as he came apart in my arms. I loved seeing him like that, seeing him all spent and tired for me, a sleepy, sated smile pulling at my favorite pair of lips.

I groaned when my cock hardened in my jeans. I needed to fucking focus on what the hell I was doing before I accidentally hammered my damn finger and ended up back in the ER.

"You look a bit distracted today, boss man," Jax teased as he leaned against a support beam, his arms crossed over his chest. "I called lunch five minutes ago."

Fuck. He wasn't wrong. I was distracted. I was distracted by my boy, but not just that. Since I'd gotten out of the hospital, narrowly escaping what could have been death, I'd been rolling an idea around in my head, wondering how best to go about it.

I wanted to marry Brayden, and I wanted to marry him soon. I wanted to give him his dream wedding, including the white dress, since he'd mentioned a couple of times when he got married, he wanted to feel like a princess—dress and all. And I'd never fucking deny him of that.

In fact, the mere image of me pushing his dress up and sinking inside his tight ass had me groaning.

Fucking hell.

Jax snorted. "Alright, brother. Talk. What's going on? You're never like this on a job. I lost count of the number of times I thought you were going to put a nail through your hand."

I grimaced and set my hammer down before scrubbing my hand down my sweaty face. "Sorry, man. Fucking got some shit on my mind."

"Well, spill it, because obviously, whatever it is, you're indecisive about it." I cut my best friend a dark look, but he just shrugged at me.

I sighed. "I want to ask Brayden to marry me." Jax didn't look the least bit surprised. Instead, a knowing smirk pulled at his lips. I punched his arm, making him scowl. He reached up to rub it. "I don't want to fuck this up, Jax. I need it to be perfect."

He sighed. "I think you're worrying too

much, Forrest. That boy loves you with every fiber of his soul. His world doesn't revolve around you; it *is* you. Nothing you do could ever fuck up that proposal for him."

I blew out a soft breath, making my way to my truck with him following beside me. "Do you think a dinner at his favorite restaurant would be nice enough?" I asked him, reaching in to grab the lunch Brayden made me the night before.

Jax nodded. "I asked Tyson to marry me with my cock buried in his ass, so I'm pretty sure your boy would be ecstatic to be proposed to in his favorite restaurant."

I barked out a laugh at that reminder. Tyson had happily said yes, but he was mortified every time Jax told anyone how they'd gotten engaged.

"I need to make some phone calls," I told Jax. "Thanks for the help, brother."

He nodded and walked off to his own truck, already pulling his phone out of his pocket, no doubt to call Tyson, his husband, and spread the news that I was finally asking Brayden to marry me.

CHAPTER NINE

Brayden

I brushed my hands over my button-down shirt, hoping it was nice enough for wherever Forrest was taking me tonight. He'd come home, kissed me to the point I was ready to beg him to fuck me, and then told me to get ready to go to a nice restaurant—that we were having a date night tonight.

"Baby boy, you look perfect," Daddy assured me, stopping behind me in the mirror. His massive body easily dwarfed mine, making me feel small but extremely loved and protected. His hands settled on my hips, and he drew me back against him. I gasped when I felt his cock press against my ass, my snug slacks assuring I felt every bit of him pressed against me through his towel.

His beard scratched my skin as he pressed a kiss to my throat. "I could just eat you up," he rasped.

I moaned, unable to tear my eyes away from the image of us reflected at me. Reaching up, he gripped my chin and turned my head, pressing a hot kiss to my lips. I moaned, opening my mouth beneath his, allowing him to thrust his tongue into my mouth, tracing every curve there.

He pulled back all too soon, leaving me panting and breathless—and so, so damn hard.

Without a word, he slipped into the walk-in closet. I took a seat on the bed, trying to get my raging hard-on under control so I wouldn't go in there and beg him to bend me over the nearest surface and fuck me until all I could remember was that he was my God, as he so often reminded me.

My cheeks flushed. Jeez, I needed to get a grip on myself. I was twenty-five years old, not a preteen who just learned that it felt good when I touched my dick.

Daddy stepped out of the closet, and my breath caught in my throat at the sight of him. He was wearing what looked to be a brand new pair of jeans with his nice boots—the man wouldn't go anywhere without boots on his feet—and a plain, black, button-down shirt that was molded to his broad chest and thick arms like a second skin.

I wiped at my face to make sure I wasn't drooling. He caught my eye in the mirror and winked. "Like what you see, boy?"

"Always, Daddy," I answered without hesitation.

He grinned. "Come on," he ordered, turning to me and holding out his hand. I quickly placed mine in his, tingles racing up and down my arm from his electric touch. It was addicting and one of the many reasons I loved his touch so much. "Let's go to dinner, sweet boy."

My jaw dropped in surprise when the

waitress led us out onto the deck, where no one else was, surprisingly. Candles were our only source of light, and rose petals were scattered on my seat and the table. Tears burned in my eyes.

"Daddy?" I croaked, looking up at the man who was my entire world.

He brushed his thumb under my eye. "While I normally love your tears, sweet boy, hold them for me until later, yeah?"

Sniffling, I nodded, my blood heating at the sensual promise in his eyes. He pulled out my chair for me, and once I was settled, he eased my chair in before taking his own, thanking the waitress when she said she'd be back with our wine.

"We don't need to order?" I asked in confusion.

Daddy laughed. "Sweet boy, I've already got everything in order. I want tonight to be extra special for you. Besides, this is your favorite restaurant. Not hard to pick what you want to eat," he lightly teased.

I flushed and then reached across the table, grabbing his hand in mine. "Thank you for being so perfect, Daddy."

He shook his head, his dark eyes intent on mine. "Brayden, I'm not perfect by any means. I just want you to be happy. Are you happy?"

I quickly nodded my head. "I've never been happier," I promised him, squeezing his hands. "You're everything to me, Daddy."

He swallowed thickly. "Even when I struggle to let you touch me?" he asked.

My heart cracked in my chest for him. There was so much raw vulnerability in that question, and it physically hurt me to hear it, especially from someone as strong as he was.

His parents had been abusive, and they'd left numerous mental scars. I knew sometimes, he still struggled to sleep, even after going through therapy. But I would never—could never—fault him for that. His struggles were not his fault.

"Daddy, I just need *you*. We will work through all of that every day like we always do. The only thing that would hurt me, Daddy, is not having you."

He reached across the table and cupped my cheek, brushing his thumb over my cheekbone and beneath my eye. "Oh, my sweet boy," he whispered. "I don't deserve you."

I shook my head. "You deserve everything in the world, Daddy."

He just smiled at me, and that smile tipped my world on its axis, just as it had done the very first time he'd smiled at me when he stepped into the salon, his hair and beard unruly and in desperate need of a cut.

The waitress popped back up with our wine and our food, and our conversation dropped, though the air of love and adoration never left the table, never left us. Daddy snuck heated, loving glances at me, constantly making me squirm. And when he would wrap his lips around his fork, his eyes intent on mine, my cock would throb with need.

"Come here," Daddy ordered once our food was cleared and the bill was paid, leaving us to ourselves in the peaceful, quiet atmosphere.

I quickly scrambled up from my chair and settled on his lap. Daddy wrapped an arm around me, and with his other hand, he held up a velvet box, a beautiful, diamond ring glistening at me. I gasped, my eyes widening all while welling up with tears.

Daddy brushed my curls back from my face before gently pressing his fingers into my chin and turning my head to face him. "I love you, baby boy. You're my entire world, the reason I breathe, and I can't imagine doing any more of this life without you. I want you forever, Brayden. And I don't mean just until death does us part. I want to find you in every life after this one and make you fall in love with me all over again."

I sobbed, my vision so blurry with tears that I could barely make out his face. I swiped at my eyes. "Will you marry me, my sweet boy? Will you spend eternity allowing me to find you in every life after this one? Will you still be mine even long after our souls stop being brought back into this world?"

I nodded. "Yes," I croaked. "Yes, Daddy. Yes. Please," I begged.

He slid the ring onto my finger and then tangled his hand in my curls, drawing my mouth to his in a hot, needy kiss.

"Home," I begged him, my hands pawing

at his shirt, needing his naked skin. "Take me home," I begged.

With a growl, he stood from the chair, my body wrapped around his, and not giving a shit about the stares we received as he walked me through the restaurant, he carried me out to the truck, his hands never stopping their exploration of my body.

CHAPTER TEN

Forrest

I groaned as Brayden unbuckled my belt and undid the button on my jeans before sliding his hand inside, wrapping it around my cock. I tightened my hands on the steering wheel, trying to focus on getting us home safely. We weren't far, only a couple more minutes left, but apparently, my boy had grown impatient.

"You're so hard, Daddy," he whispered, leaning over to press his lips to my throat.

"And I'm going to wreck your throat when we get home," I promised him, my voice barely more than a growl. "Good boys don't tease their Daddies."

He giggled, and my heart skipped a beat in my chest. "Even you said good boys can be naughty in good ways," he reminded me.

I groaned, turning on our street. "They can get punished in good ways, too, little one."

He moaned at the sensual promise in my voice, his hand tightening around my shaft. I sucked in a sharp breath, precum leaking from my cock. This boy was destroying my willpower. And thank God the house was right up ahead because I was seconds away from pulling over and seating his ass on my cock.

I threw the truck in park in the driveway and then grabbed the back of his neck, sealing my lips over his. "Bed. Now," I growled.

Giggling, he jumped out of the truck and rushed up to the house, quickly unlocking the door and then rushing inside. I slowly followed him, giving him time to get on the bed for me, and if he wasn't naked, I was going to paint his pretty little ass red for being even more of a tease and making me wait even longer to be inside of him.

I made sure he could hear my boots coming up the stairs, slow and steady. When I stepped into our bedroom, he was naked and laid out on the bed, his fingers already slicked with lube, prepping himself. I groaned at the sight, my cock jerking in my jeans.

"So beautiful, baby boy," I praised. "You ready for Daddy?" I asked him, slowly working on the buttons of my shirt as I toed my boots off.

"Almost, Daddy," he panted, moaning as he brushed that sweet spot inside of him. He sucked in a sharp breath, rocking onto his hand, his dick leaking precum onto his belly. I continued watching him as he added a third finger. He moaned and whimpered my name.

"Oh, God," he gasped when he brushed against that spot inside of him again.

"That's right, boy," I rasped, letting my shirt drop off my shoulders and hit the floor. "Call out for me. I'll answer all your prayers soon enough," I promised.

He whimpered and whined, his eyes

rolling back in his head. My jeans went next, and within the next few seconds, I was completely naked and striding toward him. Snatching the bottle of lube off the bed, I slicked my cock up and then swatted his hand away. He quickly wrapped his hand around the back of his other knee, pulling both legs up and back as far as he could for me, spreading himself open wide.

"Such a good boy," I crooned, running my hands over his thighs. Then, I positioned my cock and pushed past that first tight ring of muscle before sliding all the way inside of him. He arched his back, crying out my name, his body trembling, tears already leaking from those pretty, blue eyes.

"You better pray to me, boy, because I'm about to wreck you," I promised.

And then, I fucked him hard, fast, driving into him with enough force that I knew his ass would have bruises from my thighs pushing against him. I clawed at his hips and waist, digging my fingers into his body as I screwed up inside of him, fucking him like our lives depended on it.

I felt like I couldn't get close enough to him, couldn't get deep enough.

"Daddy!" he screamed, his cock spurting cum all over his little body, gasps ripping from his throat as he tried to breathe through his orgasm.

"Need more from you, baby boy," I growled, grabbing his cock in my hand. With a couple of strokes, he hardened again, whimpering, those baby blues locked on my face. "Can you give me more, Brayden?"

He nodded. Letting his legs drop, he circled them around my waist and then reached for me. I gripped his waist and lifted him off the bed, and pressing him against the nearest wall, I hammered up into his body, using my hands on his waist to drive him down onto me.

His screams and begs for his God had my blood pounding hot in my veins, and not wanting my boy to suffer any longer, I pressed him into the wall, plastering my body to his, allowing the friction between my stomach and his cock to get him off for me a second time.

Surprising the fuck out of me, he sank his

teeth into my shoulder as he came a second time. I slammed my hands against the wall beside his head and roared his name as I shot my cum deep inside him, marking my boy as mine for the umpteenth time.

EPILOGUE

Brayden

Nessa stepped back, nodding her head in approval at whatever she'd done to my face. "Done!" she exclaimed. I quickly got up, my dress rustling as I made my way to the mirror. She'd added mascara to my lashes, making them longer, and it was obviously the darkest color of mascara she could find because my blue eyes were popping. Light, clear lip gloss painted my lips, and she'd added a light covering of blush to my cheeks.

My hair was silver to match the wedding theme of blue and silver. I wasn't wearing heels and had instead opted to go barefoot, not wanting to be taller. I loved being short, loved standing next to my Daddy and having him tower over me, leaving me feeling protected and secure.

"Forrest is going to fall to his knees when he sees you," Tyson gushed.

He was my bridesmaid, Nessa my maid of honor. Tyson was wearing a blue suit with a silver neck tie. I knew he liked to wear dresses, too, but he'd refused to wear one today, wanting all of the attention to be on me.

"You really think he'll like me like this?" I asked, extremely nervous. He'd given me my dream wedding, including the freedom of buying a wedding dress. He'd even found an LGBTQIA+ positive wedding dress shop so I wouldn't be nervous buying a wedding dress. In fact, the moment I'd walked into the bridal dress shop, the associates there had fawned over me, leaving me feeling positively giddy and excited.

I had no idea how I'd gotten so lucky to have Daddy in my life, but I'd never take him for granted. Of that, I was certain. And I'd search for him in every life after this one to make sure we'd be reunited once again.

"It's time," my mom announced, poking her head into the room. Then, she gasped, her hands flying up to her cheeks. "Oh, Brayden, you're so beautiful!" she squealed, rushing forward to get a closer look.

My entire body burned red at her praise. "Do you think Dad will have a problem?" I asked her.

She scoffed and shook her head. "Has your father ever had an issue with anything you do, Brayden?" I shook my head because she was right. When I'd come out as gay, Dad had simply fist-bumped me and then asked if I was ready to watch the movie he'd rented.

My parents were the definition of what parental love was supposed to be like. They one hundred percent supported me. Even when they overheard me calling Forrest Daddy, they hadn't batted an eye.

"Come on," she urged, leading me from the room. "Your father is ready to walk you down the aisle."

I quickly followed her, holding up the ends of my dress along the way so I wouldn't accidentally trip. Dad arched his brows at me and released a low whistle. "Think your Daddy is going to be able to keep his hands off you?" he teased.

I flushed red and smacked his arm. "Don't be weird, Dad."

Dad just snorted and held his bent arm out to me. I placed my hand in the crook of his elbow, drawing in a deep, steady breath.

Today, I was marrying the love of my life.

Once we were in our places, the wedding march began. And when I was finally able to walk out through the curtain concealing me, a hush fell over the crowd. My eyes locked on Daddy, and I was shocked to see a tear roll down his cheek as he stared at me.

I rapidly blinked, trying not to cry, too. It would ruin my make-up, and I was deter-mined to look perfect all day, no matter how much my Daddy loved my tears.

Dad handed me over to Forrest, and my fiancé helped me up the steps to the alter. "You're fucking stunning, sweet boy."

I flushed. "Daddy, we're in church," I hissed, reprimanding him for cursing.

He flashed me a wicked grin. "Need me to

remind you of who's your God?" he softly asked, just low enough for me to hear.

Thank God I was wearing a pair of panties that would hide my hardening cock because Daddy knew just how to work me up, and I *knew* he wouldn't be able to resist doing so today.

My cheeks heated even more, making him release a husky chuckle. "You're mine later," he promised.

I was his forever.

I squeaked in alarm when the bathroom door slid open. I flung around to face my Daddy, his eyes intent on me. I swallowed thickly. "Daddy, you have to wait your turn," I hissed.

He hummed. "Thought it would be fitting to have you scream for your God while in a church," he rumbled.

Oh, fuck me.

He prowled toward me, and I backed up until I hit the bathroom counter. Daddy spun me around to face the mirror, his eyes gleaming with predatory intent. A shiver wracked through my body, my cock leaking precum. I needed him inside me so bad.

He grabbed a packet of lube out of his pocket and set it on the counter. Then, he began bunching my dress around my waist, a hiss leaving his lips at the sight of my panties. "Pretty," he hummed.

And then, he ripped them off, the lace shredding, before stuffing them in his pocket. I gasped, my eyes wide as I watched him in the mirror. He hungrily ran his over me before he roughly squeezed my ass cheeks, making me moan.

"Daddy," I whimpered.

He grabbed the packet of lube and ripped it open before slathering it all over his cock. "Are you prepped, boy, or do I need to do it for you?" he asked, always careful about not hurting me by entering me before I was ready.

"I'm ready," I panted. I'd had a feeling he wouldn't wait until after the reception to get inside of me. He could barely resist me as it was.

He eased inside of me, and I bared down,

making it easier to accommodate his massive cock. Once he was settled fully inside of me, I pushed back, needing more.

A knock sounded on the door, and I squeaked, my eyes widening in alarm. "Someone in there?" Jax called.

"Fuck off," Daddy growled at his best friend.

Jax roared with laughter before I could hear his footsteps retreating. My cheeks flamed red. I'd never be able to look at Jax the same again—not when he knew I'd gotten railed in the bathroom of a church.

"Hold on," Daddy warned.

He hammered into me. I cried out, my palms flattening against the mirror so I could lock my elbows, keeping my hips from slamming into the bathroom counter. Daddy grunted, pumping inside of me over and over with hard, bruising thrusts that had me crying out for him, desperate for more— always wanting more from him.

"God," I sobbed, tears running down my cheeks, ruining my make-up.

"You cry so prettily for me," Daddy rasped, reaching forward to grip my chin, forcing me to watch him fuck me in the mirror. And that was all it took. I came undone, screaming his name as I painted the tile floor beneath us with my cum.

Daddy growled my name, his grip tightening on my hips as he spilled inside of me. My chest heaved as I slumped on the counter, my knees feeling weak. I winced as Daddy eased out of me, and then he crouched behind me, sinking his tongue into my ass.

"Oh, God," I whimpered.

"That's right, baby boy. *I'm* your God," he swore before he began to clean up his mess, bringing me to yet another orgasm.

ALSO BY WEST GREENE

Want to stay up-to-date with sales, new releases, new preorders, etc?

Join my newsletter!

https://westgreenebooks.com

Facebook

Instagram

Facebook Group

Mastadon

Twitter

Patreon

Pinterest

Access my merch store here.

ABOUT THE AUTHOR

West Greene is a romance author that specializes in short, steamy books and erotic shorts.

All your instalove needs can be found in one of her books, whether you're looking for possessive men, men with no morals, spicy FF romance, a boy just needing his Daddy, a twink just needing love, or even the other woman to get her HEA.

West Greene refuses to be stuck in one trope or type of romance. She loves variety, and she's definitely going to share that variety with her readers.